Christina's love for storytelling and illustrations stem from the classic fairy tales she grew up on. Her whimsical outlook keeps her inner-child alive in creating funny stories adults and children can enjoy. Christina currently resides in Chandler, Indiana with her husband and a little monster.

DAT DARE
MONSTER

by
Christina M. Mizerak

AUSTIN MACAULEY PUBLISHERS™
LONDON • CAMBRIDGE • NEW YORK • SHARJAH

Copyright © Christina M. Mizerak (2019)

Ordering Information:
Quantity sales: special discounts are available on quantity purchases by corporations, associations, and others. For details, contact the publisher at the address below.

Mizerak, Christina M.
Dat Dare Monster

ISBN 9781641828604 (Paperback)
ISBN 9781641828611 (Hardback)
ISBN 9781641828628 (E-Book)

The main category of the book — JUVENILE FICTION / Ghost Stories

www.austinmacauley.com/us

First Published (2019)
Austin Macauley Publishers LLC
40 Wall Street, 28th Floor
New York, NY 10005

USA
mail-usa@austinmacauley.com
+1 (646) 5125767

To my loving husband who keeps the scary monsters away.

All my love to my parents for always supporting my dreams, and Melissa for inspiring me to go for it!

Did I ever tell you about
when I was kidnapped?
Yes sir, a monster stole me
right out of my room.

8

It was a few days ago. I was playing dollies in my room when dat dare monster grabbed my leg.
I shouted, "No!" and "Stop dat. Let me go!"

He backed up quick and whimpered like a dog. He looked mighty sad.

I got down real low on my tummy and reached for him. I felt bad, see, and wanted to apologize. Dat dare monster grabbed my arm and pulled me under! I tried to get away, but he held on tight.

Deep under my bed we went. Dare's so much under dare.
My blocks, bouncy balls, and Mr. Snorts, duh piggy were dare.

14

Dat dare monster pulled me on. Den, dare was a door. A big, bright, blue door! Inside dat door was a table. On dat table was a tea party.

Dat dare monster offered me
a chair wid a sweet smile. I
sat down and waited.
Dat dare monster poured tea
and served cake.
We sat and laughed, chit
chatting about dis and dat.
Dat dare monster was a
funny dude.

18

After tea, we danced and
sang until I was exhausted.

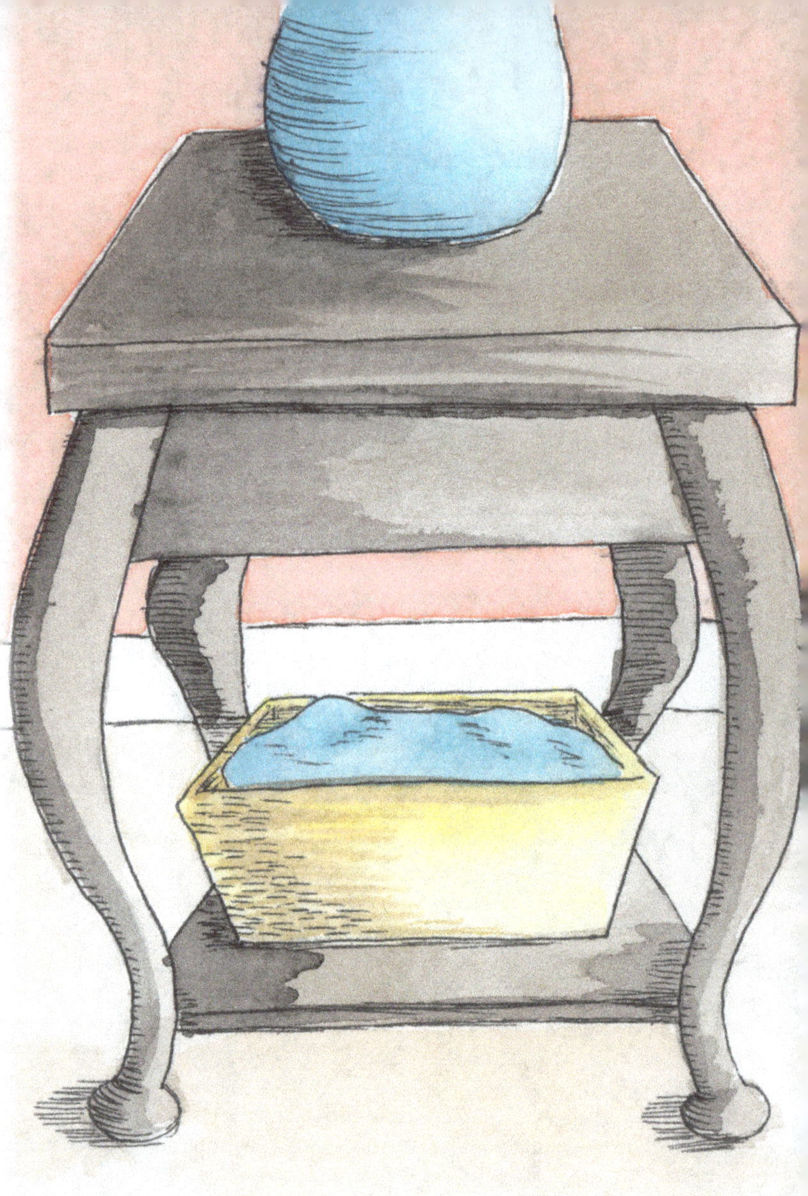

I laid down to rest for a while. Do you know what happened den? Dat dare monster returned me to my room! Yes sir, he did.

When I woke up, I climbed under my bed for dat dare monster, but all I found were blocks, bouncy balls, and Mr. Snorts, duh piggy. No big, bright, blue door or nudding.

I dink he went on vacation,
dat dare monster.